LEGO friends

ULTIMATE STICKER COLLECTION

How to use this book

Read the captions, then find
the sticker that best fits the space.
(Hint: check the sticker labels for clues!)

•

Don't forget that your stickers can
be stuck down and peeled off again.

•

There are lots of fantastic extra stickers for
creating your own scenes throughout the book.

DK

LONDON, NEW YORK,
MELBOURNE, MUNICH, AND DELHI

Written by Beth Landis Hester
Edited by Elizabeth Dowsett and Helen Murray
Designed for DK by Lisa Robb
Cover designed by Lauren Rosier

Published in the United States
in 2013 by DK Publishing
375 Hudson Street, New York, New York 10014

10 9 8 7 6 5 4 3 2 1

001–182981–Mar/13

Page design copyright © 2013 Dorling Kindersley Limited

Published in Great Britain by Dorling Kindersley Limited.

DK books are available at special discounts when purchased in bulk for sales
promotions, premiums, fund-raising, or educational use.
For details contact:
DK Publishing Special Markets
375 Hudson Street
New York, New York 10014
SpecialSales@dk.com

A CIP catalog record for this book is available from the Library of Congress.

ISBN: 978-1-4654-0178-6

Color Reproduction by Altaimage in the UK
Printed and bound in China by L-Rex

Discover more at
www.dk.com
www.LEGO.com

Meet the Friends

What's the best thing of all about Heartlake City? The amazing friends who live there, of course! Each of the girls is special and unique, but every single one is loyal, friendly, and lots of fun. They are such good friends, they have even created a Friends Club to help others!

Emma

Emma photographs the things that inspire her. She uses her favorite colors and shapes to inspire new fashion designs!

Olivia

Clever Olivia loves to solve problems and discover new facts. In her workshop, she comes up with new inventions.

Andrea

Wherever there's a stage, Andrea will hop up and sing! She loves to perform for her biggest fans: her four best friends.

Stephanie

Sociable Stephanie loves helping out friends, and never forgets a birthday! As a Pet Patrol volunteer, she helps animals, too.

Mia

Mia has a way with animals and takes care of all her pets. At Heartlake Vet, she's also learning to care for other animals.

Ella

Ella loves riding, helping out at the stables, and exploring horse trails in the woods—anything that involves horses!

Katharina

Look for Katharina at the stables. If she's not practicing for her next big show, she may be grooming her favorite horse, Niki.

Nicole

Adventurous Nicole is the perfect companion for a camping trip or a hike! She loves exploring nature with friends.

Treehouse HQ

This is the Friends Club headquarters! It is fixed up as a girls-only hangout for sunny days and starry nights.

Heartlake City

Heartlake City is a wonderful place to live. It has everything a girl could want! Olivia, Emma, Stephanie, Andrea, and Mia are lucky to call it home. They always find lots of exciting places to visit and cozy spots to hang out. Start your tour here . . . then enjoy exploring!

©2013 LEGO

Flying Club

Spread your wings at Heartlake City's Flying Club. Just a few exciting lessons and you'll soar up, up, and away!

©2013 LEGO

©2013 LEGO

Heartlake Stables

Horseback riding is an exciting way to spend an afternoon. Visit the horses at the stables or take a trail ride!

Vet's office

This is where Sophie the vet cares for horses with sore hooves, lost puppies, and even a hedgehog with a cold!

Cruising

Who's ready for a road trip? Emma's car is a cool way to tour the coast or mountains near Heartlake City.

City Park Café

Take a snack break! The outdoor tables at City Park Café are a comfy place to catch up with friends.

Café

©2013 LEGO

©2013 LEGO

Create your own scene

Fill this scene with all the fun and exciting ways to spend time in Heartlake City.

5

Olivia

Olivia is adventurous, smart, and practical. And she's excited to meet new friends! She just moved to a beautiful new home in Heartlake City with her mom, dad, and cat Kitty.

Budding scientist

Science is one of Olivia's favorite subjects. She loves to do experiments and figure out for herself how things work.

Olivia's diary

Olivia fills her diary with stories about her adventures and best friends. In Heartlake City, there is always something to write about!

Zobo the robot

Olivia has a talent for inventing. She built her pet robot herself! A remote control makes him go.

Anna

Olivia's mom is a kind, caring doctor. Her patients at the hospital love her almost as much as her family does!

Backyard swing

This quiet spot is Olivia's favorite place to sit and think. There's no better perch for enjoying the beautiful backyard.

©2013 LEGO

Peter

Olivia's dad is a newspaper editor. He is also a great cook. He has a grill set up in the backyard for delicious outdoor family meals.

©2013 LEGO

©2013 LEGO

Home sweet home

Peter, Anna, and Olivia live in a big home with a pretty garden and roof terrace. Their address is #30, Heartlake Heights.

©2013 LEGO

Schoolwork first

Olivia loves to learn new things. Her colorful desk is a cheerful spot to study her favorite school subjects: art, history, and science.

©2013 LEGO

Inventor's workshop

Olivia's microscope helps her see her experiments up close. She also has a workbench where she builds her latest inventions.

7

Andrea

Outgoing Andrea was born to be a star! She loves sharing her talent for dancing, acting, and especially singing. Andrea sings all the time—on stage, at work, and even in the shower!

On stage

Bubbly Andrea is right at home in the spotlight. Her friends are there to cheer her on whenever she takes to the stage.

©2013 LEGO

©2013 LEGO

Singing star

Andrea dreams of singing for huge audiences. She's sure to be a superstar someday!

Piano practice

Playing piano takes hard work, but it's worth it! It's so much fun to be able to play all your favorite songs.

©2013 LEGO

©2013 LEGO

Bunny house

Andrea thinks that caring for animals is lots of fun—especially when they are as cute as her little bunny Jazz!

Stargazing

As well as wanting to be a star herself, Andrea also likes using her telescope to spot real stars in the night sky.

Tasty work

What's the best part of working at the café? Taste testing! Andrea gets to try every treat on the menu.

Serving food

At the café, Andrea's job is to bring the customers their drinks and snacks. But she always finds time to sing a little, too!

Carrot treat

Leftover food from the café makes a perfect snack for pets. This carrot goes right to the bunny house.

Building sandcastles

The sounds of the waves and seagulls at the beach inspire some of Andrea's music . . . and her sandcastles, too!

©2013 LEGO

9

Emma

Emma has an eye for design. She keeps up with the latest trends and finds inspiration everywhere. She loves helping her friends add style to their lives. They love hearing her declare, "That's so you!"

Sweet treat

Emma's favorite dessert is a yummy milkshake from the café. A mix of two flavors is her one-of-a-kind blend.

Ready to ride

Emma is a champion horseback rider! She puts on her riding hat and is all set to go to a competition with her horse Robin.

Fashion designer

Emma mixes patterns and colors for original outfits. She measures each piece carefully so the fit is just right.

Drawing board

This style board lets Emma mix and match design ideas. She can change up the pictures until the outfit is perfect.

Shutterbug Emma

Emma always keeps a camera handy to snap pictures around Heartlake City. You never know where creativity will strike!

©2013 LEGO

10

Cool pool

This splash pool is a cool spot on hot days! Emma sits in the refreshing water to feel relaxed and chilled out.

©2013 LEGO

Cute hedgehog

This little critter is well cared for by gentle Emma. Sometimes she even decorates him with bows, too!

©2013 LEGO

Music to go

Emma loves to listen to music when she's out and about. Her MP3 player is loaded with all her favorite songs.

©2013 LEGO

Computer research

Emma logs on to her laptop to find out about the latest fashion trends. There's always something new to learn!

©2013 LEGO

11

Mia

Kindhearted Mia loves animals. They seem to understand her when she talks to them! Mia is a vegetarian, which means she never eats meat, and she hopes to become an animal doctor when she grows up.

Drum practice

Mia loves to drum! She always plays far away from the animals so they aren't frightened by the loud noise.

©2013 LEGO

Puppy house

Mia is a terrific animal trainer. Charlie's doghouse is decorated with the ribbons he's won at the Heartlake City Dog Show.

©2013 LEGO

Budding vet

Mia helps out at the vet's office whenever she can. Mischievous puppy Scarlett has hopped on to the rescue trolley for a ride!

Sophie

Olivia's aunt is Heartlake City's top veterinarian. She's teaching Mia how to care for all kinds of animals.

©2013 LEGO

©2013 LEGO

Bella

Mia's horse is a champion show jumper! Bella also loves to go for long runs with her favorite rider.

©2013 LEGO

©2013 LEGO

Favorite visitor

Mia visits Bella every morning and evening. She always has a kind word for her horse, and Bella loves to listen!

©2013 LEGO

Niki

Tasty apple

Generous Mia is happy to share treats with all her animal friends. Bella's neighbor Niki will enjoy this crunchy apple!

Diary writing

In her journal, Mia writes about her adventures, her friends, and her dreams of one day becoming a vet.

©2013 LEGO

13

Stephanie

Mia's cousin Stephanie is lots of fun to be around. She is great at organizing activities and cool parties! She knows just about everyone in Heartlake City and always has a bright smile for her many friends.

Looking good
Stephanie likes to have everything in its place, including well-brushed hair and cute accessories!

Keen baker
Making cakes keeps Stephanie busy. When a friend has a birthday, she likes to treat them to something sweet!

Cute Coco
Stephanie's pet dog, Coco, is always carefully groomed. Plenty of brushing makes her fur shiny and soft.

Cool convertible
Stephanie can fit Coco and all her gear in this open-topped car. Now she'll turn on some tunes and hit the road.

Celebration cake
Stephanie loves to party and to celebrate her friends. She brings along cake to get everyone in the party spirit!

©2013 LEGO

14

Welcome to the Flying Club

This budding pilot can't wait for her next lesson. Watch overhead—the next plane you see might be Stephanie's!

Keep in touch!

This handwritten note is sure to bring a smile to one of Stephanie's many pen pals!

Grooming Niki

Stephanie always makes time for the horses at the stables. Her favorite horse, Niki, gets lots of attention!

Pet Patrol

Stephanie's knowledge of Heartlake City is a big help for the Pet Patrol. She'll get this lost pet home in no time!

Animal Friends

The Heartlake City friends look out for each other—and they take good care of animals, too! They have their own pets, but they are always on the lookout for other animals in need of rescue or help. Here are some of the fuzzy, feathered, and even spiny friends that the Heartlake girls love to spend time with.

Kitty

Olivia's mischievous cat finds lots of hiding places in her new Heartlake City home. Olivia always manages to find Kitty, though!

©2013 LEGO

Caretakers

The girls work hard caring for their pets. Andrea sweeps out her bunny's house before school each day.

Robin

Emma always keeps her horse, Robin, groomed and pampered. Sometimes she decorates Robin's stable so even the hay is color-coordinated!

©2013 LEGO

Scarlett

This cute puppy has been well cared for by the girls. She even got a makeover! It's hard to believe she used to be so scruffy.

Charlie

Charlie is a Heartlake City Dog Show champion! Proud Mia displays the awards at home on the doghouse.

©2013 LEGO

Goldie

Goldie had a broken wing when the girls found him near the treehouse. The friends helped nurse this bird back to health.

Maxie

This adorable cat has become a permanent resident of the treehouse! The girls even built Maxie a bed so she can sleep there.

Daisy

This bunny keeps the Pet Patrol on its toes! When Daisy hops away, Stephanie guides her home with a tasty carrot.

Oscar

There are all kinds of cute and cuddly creatures in Heartlake City. This is Oscar, the town's cutest— but not so cuddly—hedgehog!

©2013 LEGO

City Park Café

In the city park, there is a popular spot with a beautiful view of Lake Heart. This is where you'll find the busy café. With all the yummy treats on the menu and the sunny outdoor tables, it's easy to see why the friends love to hang out here!

Marie
Marie owns the café. She is an expert baker and a great boss. She greets guests with a smile and a fresh-baked treat.

Andrea the waitress
Working at the café, Andrea gets to see her friends and try all the food! Best of all, Marie lets her sing for the customers.

Cupcake
These are the café's specialty! Marie frosts each cupcake with care. Would you choose chocolate or strawberry?

Ker-ching!
The cash register holds all the day's earnings. When the café is busy, the money drawer fills up fast!

Delicious burger
Tasty sandwiches and burgers are the perfect lunch for hungry customers. There's one for every taste. Mia loves the veggie burger!

Busy baker
Marie starts baking early every morning. When customers arrive, the café is filled with the sweet smell of pies and cakes.

18

Cupcake offer!

The treat of the day is posted outside, where people walking by can see. Today's special is hard to resist!

Busy Andrea

As part of her job, Andrea takes the money from customers. She also brings food, tidies up, and, of course, sings whenever she can.

©2013 LEGO

Tidy Marie

Marie does the sweeping herself, since Andrea gets carried away singing and uses the broom as a microphone!

©2013 LEGO

Super shakes

Marie is famous for her milkshakes! They are thick, creamy, and delicious. And they come in everyone's favorite flavors.

©2013 LEGO

Café

19

Beauty Salon

For the latest fashions, everybody in Heartlake City goes to Butterfly Beauty Shop. The salon is the coolest place to get expert, personal advice on what will suit you best, whether it's a new accessory you're after or a whole new look. While you're there, why not indulge in some pampering, too?

©2013 LEGO

©2013 LEGO

Glamorous Emma

Emma is always on the lookout for pretty things. Her talent for design helps her spot the cutest fashions.

Style pro

Stylish Sarah works at the Beauty Shop. The girls love her design tips. She gives great advice about lipstick colors!

Pick and mix

There are so many cool accessories to choose from! Trying them on is the only way to see what looks best.

©2013 LEGO

Chic sunglasses

What's the quickest way to add glamour to an outfit? Top it with a pair of sunglasses! The beauty shop has lots.

©2013 LEGO

Hairdressing

Nobody can style hair like Sarah. Emma loves getting her hair done while Sarah shows her the latest styles.

©2013 LEGO

Hair accessories

After a day of pampering, a pretty bow is the perfect finishing touch to any hairstyle.

©2013 LEGO

Makeover mirror

When it's makeover time, the girls crowd around the mirror to admire each other's new looks.

New offers

The sign outside the shop promises the latest makeup ranges. Would you try this new petal-pink shade of lipstick?

Olivia's purse

The pink trimming on Olivia's new purse is a perfect match with her purple-and-pink outfit. What a great find!

Tool of the trade

A professional hairdryer gives Sarah's hairdos lots of shine and style.

©2013 LEGO

©2013 LEGO

©2013 LEGO

©2013 LEGO

Beauty Shop

At the Dog Show

With obstacle courses, judges to impress, and a flower-filled stage, the annual dog show is one of Heartlake City's biggest events. It takes a lot of dedication and careful training to get a dog ready to compete, but it's lots of fun. The Heartlake girls love to take part with their dogs.

©2013 LEGO

Mia the dog trainer

For Mia, the dog show is one of the highlights of the year. What could be better than an afternoon of animal fun?

Puppy bath

Each dog gets a good bath before going before the judges. Charlie's white coat looks best after a soak.

©2013 LEGO

Pink ribbons

Pretty ribbon prizes go to the dogs who perform best at the show. Mia is hopeful that her dog Charlie will win this one.

©2013 LEGO

Grooming basket

Bows and a brush make sure the dogs look their best while they run, climb, and jump through the obstacle course.

©2013 LEGO

Trophy time!

The lucky winners stand on the podium of honor, alongside the dog show's grand-prize trophy.

©2013 LEGO

Dog's dinner

The winning dogs get ribbons, but every dog earns a tasty bone to chew on. It is a dog's favorite prize of all!

©2013 LEGO

22

Create your own scene

Put your favorite dog show stickers here to create the best dog show Heartlake City has ever seen.

Life Outdoors

Where can you hike, swim, skate, ride, and even fly? The best city around: Heartlake City! With beaches, mountains, and pretty parks nearby, it's such an adventurous place to live. There are so many exhilarating activities, you'll find there's never a dull moment!

Home from home

This deluxe camper van is perfect for a few days vacation exploring further afield. Every night is a sleepover!

Healing hands

The girls found this poor bird who had a broken wing. Together, they nursed it back to health. Caring for living things makes them all feel good!

Skater girl

Mia feels the breeze as she whizzes by on her skateboard. Her balance is so good, she can even hold an ice cream while she rides!

Cookouts

Who says dinner has to be inside? The girls love to cook meals al fresco on this outdoor grill.

Secret stash

The girls hide their special collection of treasures, including crystals, in this box at the treehouse.

24

I spy!

A telescope at the flight school lets Stephanie take a closer look at everything in the woods below and the sky above.

©2013 LEGO

Up, up, and away!

Stephanie is learning to operate this high-flying prop plane. She can see all of Heartlake City from up here!

©2013 LEGO

©2013 LEGO

Surf's up!

When the waves are high, a surfboard is one cool ride! Hop right on and catch a wave.

©2013 LEGO

Cycling adventures

Nicole and Olivia bring a picnic on long bike rides. They can spend all day exploring the trails around Heartlake City!

Winter Fun

Winter is no reason to stay indoors in Heartlake City! Snowy days here give a whole new meaning to "cool." There are hills for sledding and skiing, and cozy fires for warming chilly toes. The whole city looks magical under a blanket of snow. How can you resist it?

Cozy clothes

The girls stay snuggly warm by bundling up! Olivia knows that lots of layers and a good pair of boots are key to keeping out the cold.

Hold tight!

At the first sign of snow, Olivia and her friends grab their sleds and start looking for the very best sledding hill.

Warming treat

After an active day outside, a cup of hot cocoa always hits the spot. Add marshmallows for a sweet topper!

Snowman

The girls love building snowmen. They use sticks to make the arms and top each snowman with a stylish hat.

©2013 LEGO

Create your own scene

How would you spend a snow day? Fill this scene with any stickers you choose!

At the Beach

Head to this sandy spot to catch a refreshing sea breeze. With the right gear, you might catch a cool wave, too! The beach has something for every mood. If you are looking for adventure, try the exciting watersports. Or if you want something more sedate, sink into the soft sand for a relaxing rest.

©2013 LEGO

Surfer girl
Olivia has been practicing her surfing all summer long. She paddles out, stands on her board, and tries not to wipe out!

©2013 LEGO

Seaside snack
Nicole remembers to bring along the picnic basket. Her favorite refresher on the beach? Orange juice!

©2013 LEGO

Fun in the sand
This sandcastle is fit for a princess! Four corner towers and a big pink flag give it an extra royal touch.

Out at sea
This powerboat zips through the waves with Olivia at the wheel. The blue windshield protects her from splashes.

Sun lounging
Olivia takes a break on her sunbed. An umbrella shades it from the sun—it's always comfy and cool underneath!

©2013 LEGO

©2013 LEGO

Create your own scene

Are you ready to hit the beach? Fill the sand with seaside stickers to set the scene.

29

Riding Camp

The end of the school year means holidays, but for some lucky girls it also means the start of riding camp! The girls pack their bags and load their horses into the trailer. Then they are off for an unforgettable summer adventure of riding and learning to care for their horses.

Bon voyage!

The girls buckle up in this bus for the journey to camp. There is plenty of room for four girls and all their gear.

Pitching in

Stephanie grabs a pitchfork to prepare the stables. She spreads fresh hay on the floor to make a bed for each horse.

Theresa

Expert rider Theresa is the camp's head counselor. She's a wonderful teacher, and great company, too!

Trail leader

Theresa leads the group on rides through the nearby pastures. She knows every trail by heart.

Grooming

Ella brushes her horse's mane, tail, and coat to keep them healthy and shiny. Like the girls, the horses love to be pampered!

Tacking up

The girls learn how to fit a horse with a saddle and bridle. Once the tack is secure, Foxy is ready to go!

In class

Indoors, Theresa teaches the girls everything there is to know about riding and looking after horses.

Fireside treats

After a day's riding, the campers chat around the fire, drink sweet cocoa, and toast gooey marshmallows. Yum!

Helping out

Emma pushes a wheelbarrow to cart a bale of hay across camp. It's good exercise—and the horses will love it!

©2013 LEGO

At the Stables

Where do Heartlake City's horses live? Beautiful Heartlake Stables! The girls love to spend time here, grooming and petting their horses. They even like to decorate the horses' stalls to make them extra pretty. But the main event, of course, is taking the horses out for a ride!

©2013 LEGO

Tasty carrot
Katharina is ready to ride! But first she offers her horse, Niki, a healthy snack to eat.

Horsey home
Bella loves her cozy stable—especially when Mia visits! Somehow Mia always seems to know what Bella needs.

Tea for two
Horseback riding can be tiring! A cup of tea or water after a ride helps the girls feel good as new.

©2013 LEGO

©2013 LEGO

Stable hand
At the stables, Mia does what she can to make sure the horses are comfortable and well fed.

©2013 LEGO

Show jumping
Leaping over rails is a thrilling challenge. It looks like Katharina and her horse have mastered this one!

©2013 LEGO

Ker-ching!

Trophy

Animal emergency

Musical Andrea

Stephanie

Fireside treats

Flying high!

Makeup

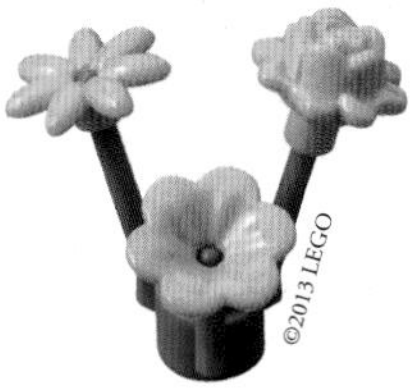

Flowers

Tacking up

Bath time

Emma

Lipstick

Seesaw

Coco

Super shakes

Treehouse HQ

Busy baker

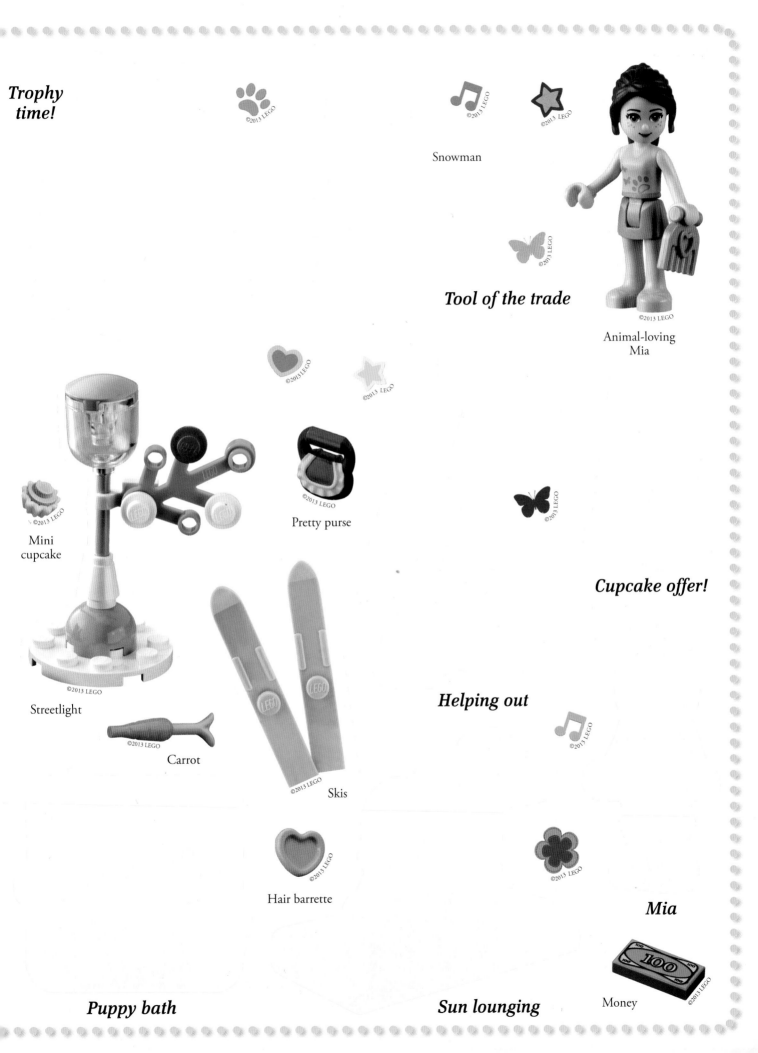

Trophy time!

Snowman

Tool of the trade

Animal-loving Mia

Mini cupcake

Pretty purse

Cupcake offer!

Streetlight

Carrot

Helping out

Skis

Hair barrette

Mia

Money

Puppy bath

Sun lounging

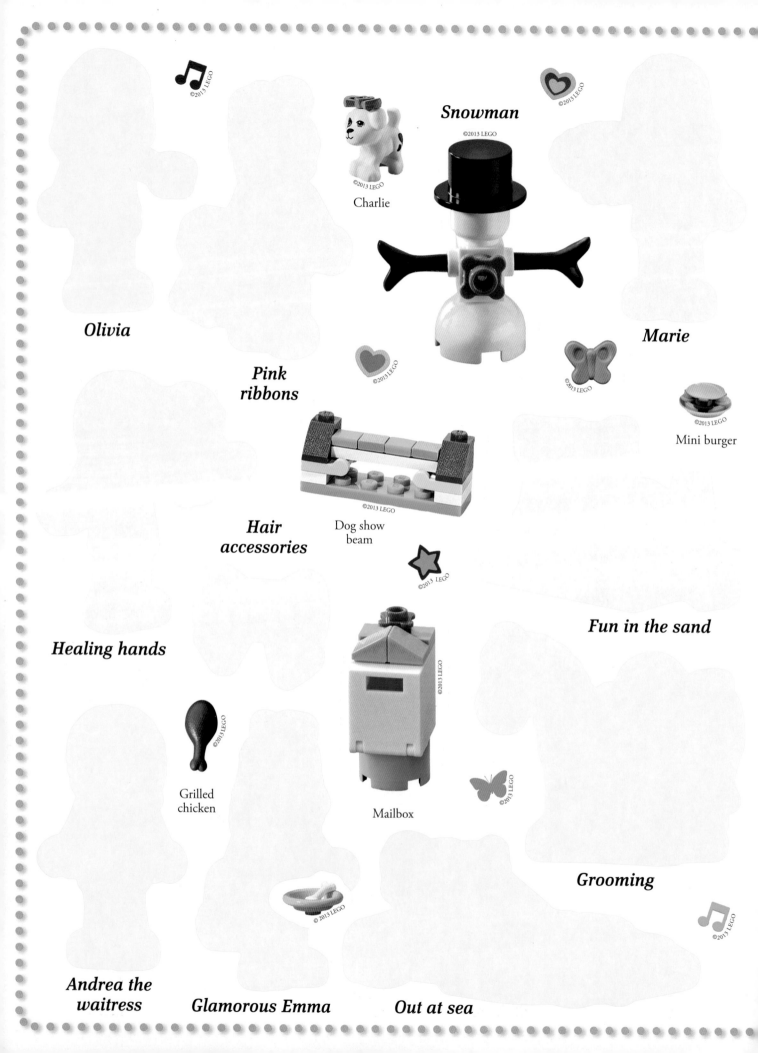

Olivia

Snowman

Charlie

Marie

Pink ribbons

Mini burger

Hair accessories

Dog show beam

Fun in the sand

Healing hands

Grilled chicken

Mailbox

Grooming

Andrea the waitress

Glamorous Emma

Out at sea

Cookouts

Cozy clothes

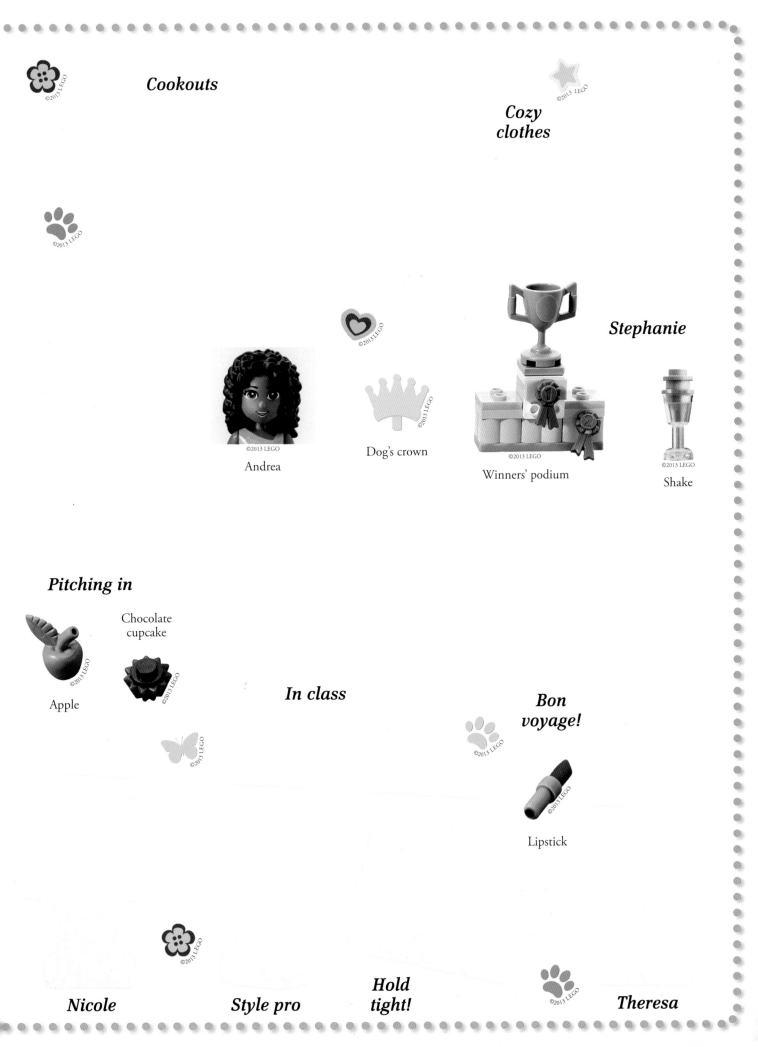

Stephanie

Andrea

Dog's crown

Winners' podium

Shake

Pitching in

Chocolate cupcake

In class

Bon voyage!

Apple

Lipstick

Nicole   *Style pro*   **Hold tight!**   *Theresa*

Trail leader

Sociable
Stephanie

Andrea

Winner's
ribbon

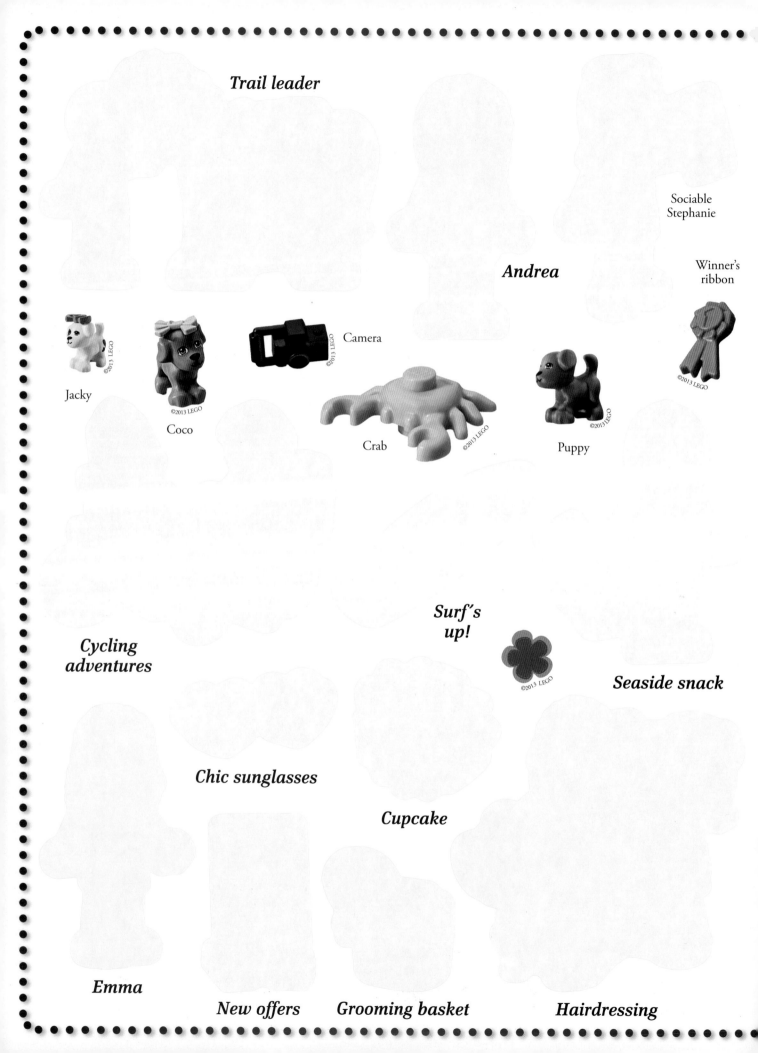

Camera

Jacky

Coco

Crab

Puppy

Cycling
adventures

Surf's
up!

Seaside snack

Chic sunglasses

Cupcake

Emma

New offers   Grooming basket   Hairdressing

Dog's dinner   *Tidy Marie*

I spy!

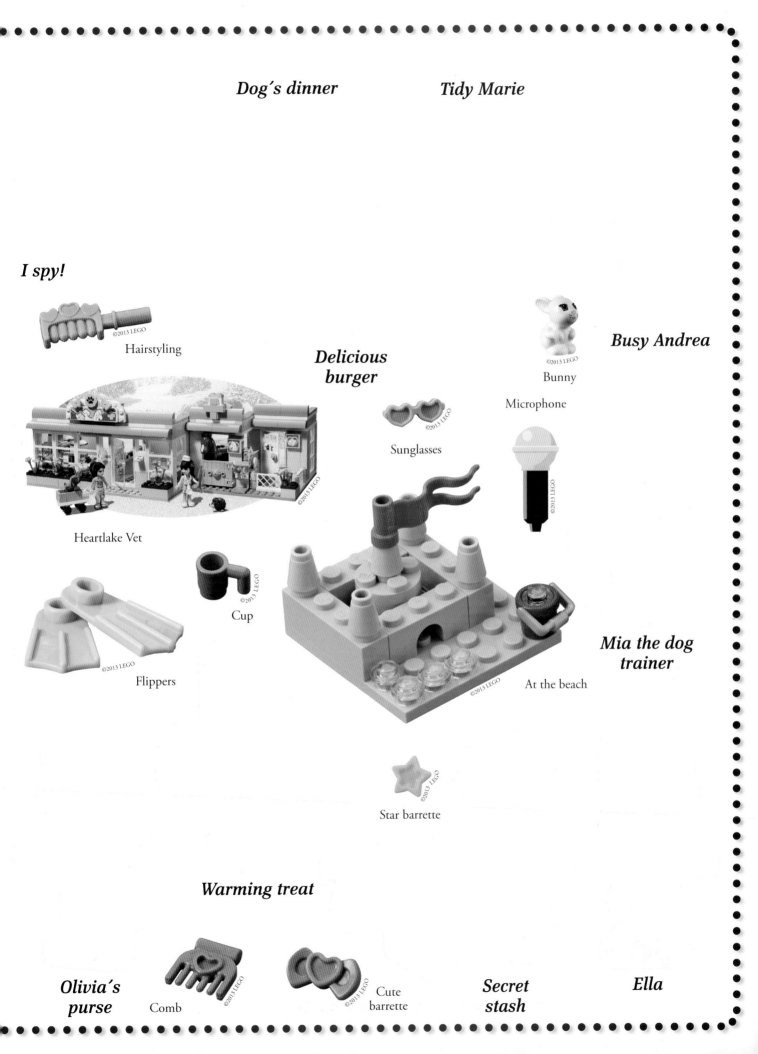

Hairstyling

Delicious burger

Bunny

Busy Andrea

Microphone

Sunglasses

Heartlake Vet

Cup

Flippers

At the beach

Mia the dog trainer

Star barrette

Warming treat

Olivia's purse   Comb   Cute barrette   *Secret stash*   *Ella*

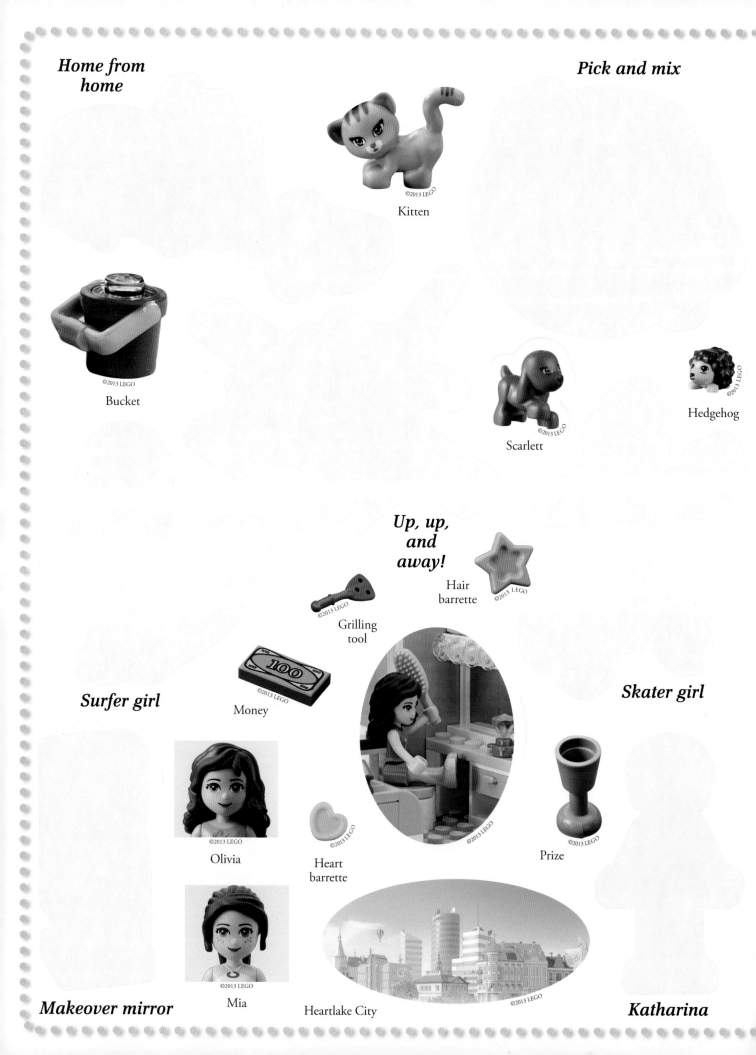

Home from home

Pick and mix

Kitten

Bucket

Scarlett

Hedgehog

Up, up, and away!

Hair barrette

Grilling tool

Money

Surfer girl

Skater girl

Olivia

Heart barrette

Prize

Makeover mirror

Mia

Heartlake City

Katharina

Drawing board

Grilling outdoors

Ice-cream sundae

Bone

Music to go

Best friends

Tasty apple

Keen baker

Tea for two

Show jumping

Stephanie's car

Singing star

Cute hedgehog

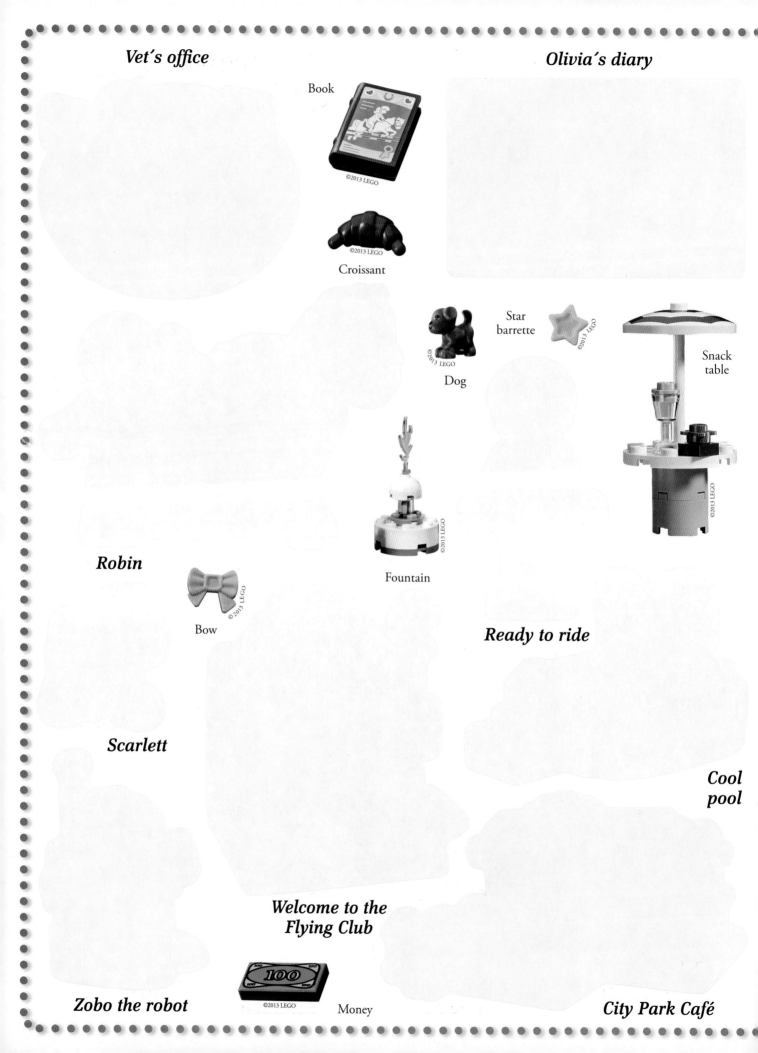

Vet's office

Olivia's diary

Book

Croissant

Star barrette

Dog

Snack table

Robin

Fountain

Ready to ride

Bow

Scarlett

Cool pool

Welcome to the Flying Club

Zobo the robot

Money

City Park Café

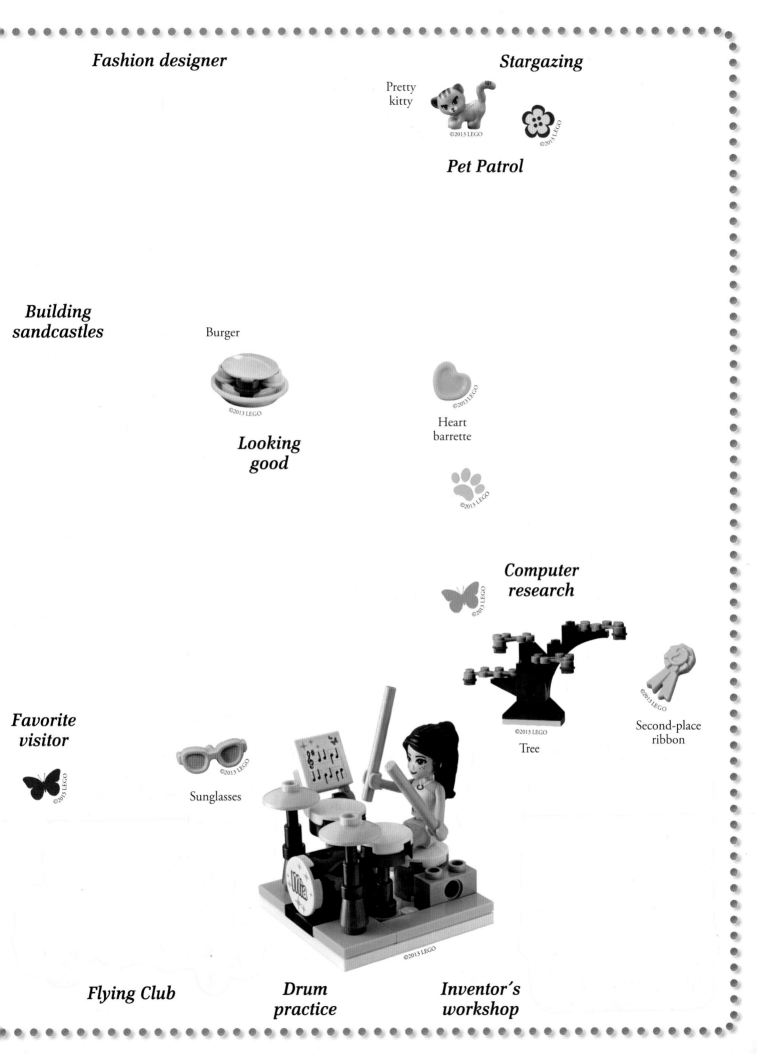

Fashion designer

Stargazing

Pretty kitty

Pet Patrol

Building sandcastles

Burger

Heart barrette

Looking good

Computer research

Favorite visitor

Sunglasses

Second-place ribbon

Tree

Flying Club

Drum practice

Inventor's workshop

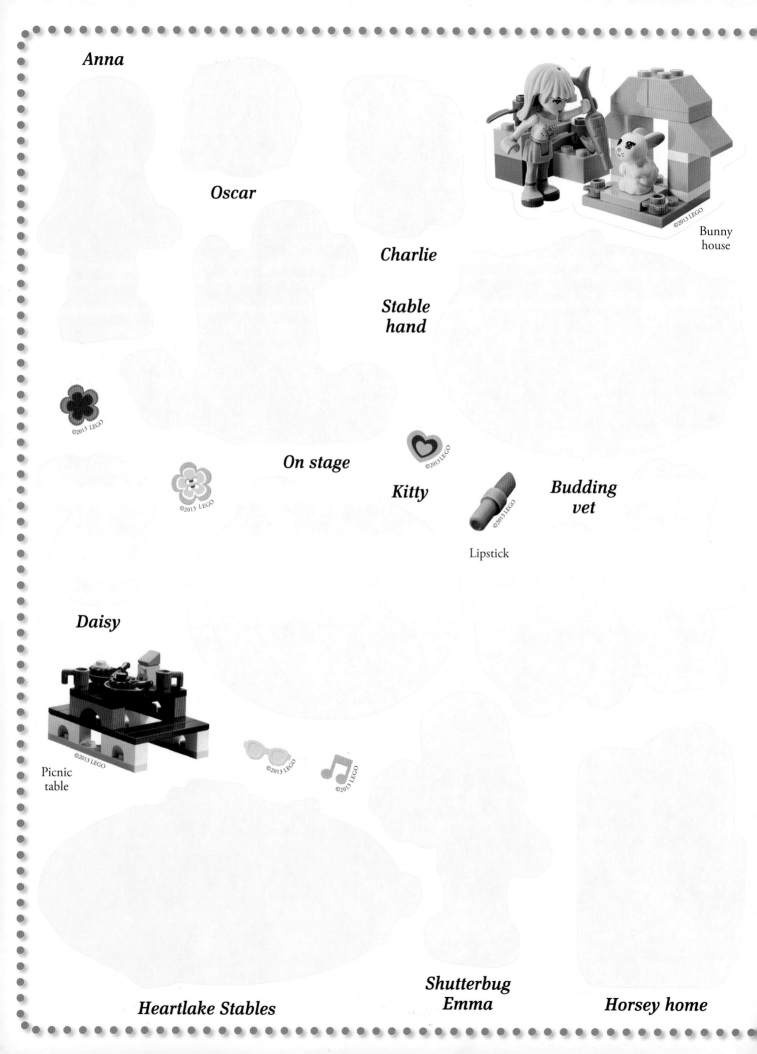

Anna

Oscar

Bunny
house

Charlie

*Stable
hand*

On stage

Kitty

*Budding
vet*

Lipstick

Daisy

Picnic
table

Heartlake Stables

*Shutterbug
Emma*

Horsey home

Sweet treat

Backyard swing

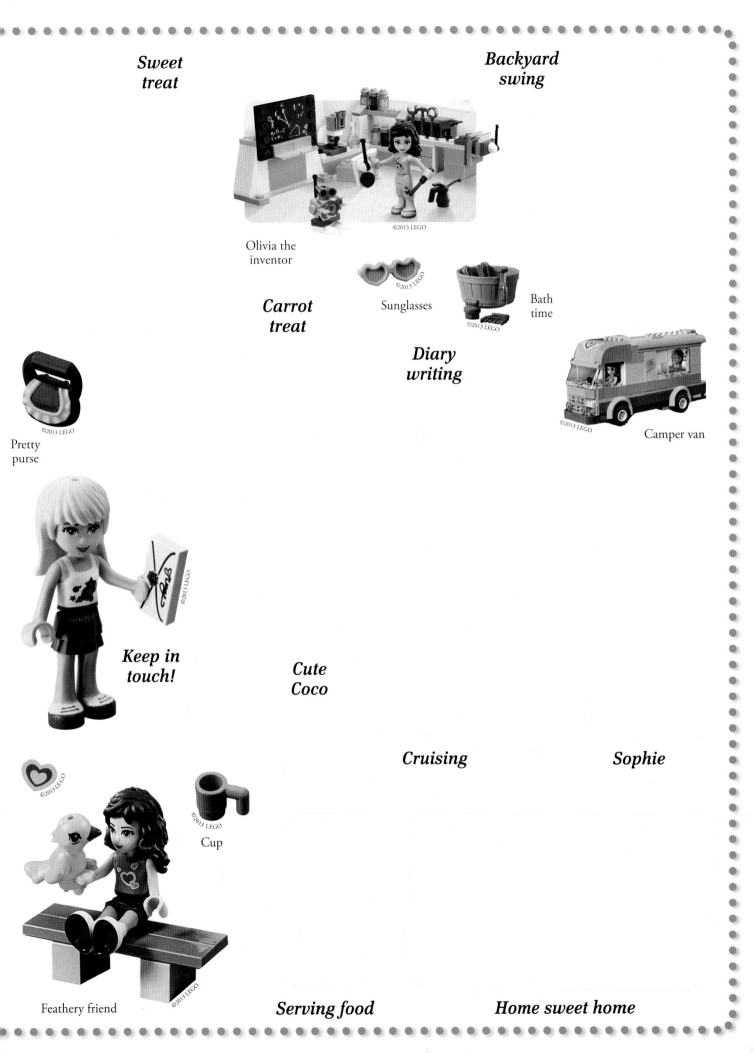

Olivia the inventor

Carrot treat

Sunglasses

Bath time

Diary writing

Camper van

Pretty purse

Keep in touch!

Cute Coco

Cruising

Sophie

Cup

Feathery friend

Serving food

Home sweet home

Bunny house

Carrot

Maxie

Peter

Flower barrette

Grilled chicken

Foxy

Relaxing on the beach

Grooming Niki

Vegetable garden

Cool convertible

Comb

Butterfly Beauty Shop

Bella

Piano practice

Tasty work

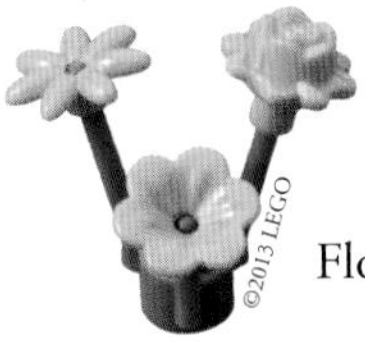

Celebration cake

Flowers

Cupcake

Flower barrette

Caretakers

Goldie

Mia's radio

Tasty carrot

Plant

Horse trailer

Lipstick

Puppy house

Schoolwork first

Budding scientist

Extra Stickers

Extra Stickers

©2013 LEGO

Extra Stickers

Extra Stickers

Extra Stickers

Extra Stickers

©2013 LEGO

Extra Stickers

©2013 LEGO

Extra Stickers

©2013 LEGO

Extra Stickers

©2013 LEGO

Extra Stickers

Extra Stickers

©2013 LEGO

Extra Stickers

©2013 LEGO

Extra Stickers

©2013 LEGO

Extra Stickers

Extra Stickers

Extra Stickers